STORYTIME COLLECTION

This book belongs to

_____

_____

Published in 2018
by Autumn Publishing
Cottage Farm
Sywell
NN6 0BJ
www.igloobooks.com

GUA009 0718
2 4 6 8 10 9 7 5 3
ISBN 978-1-78810-987-1

Printed and manufactured in China

DISNEY
M☺ANA

☺ STORYTIME COLLECTION ☺

A long time ago, on the beautiful island of Motunui, a little girl lived with her family. Her name was Moana. Her father, Tui, was chief of the island and, one day, Moana would become chief, too.

Chief Tui cared deeply for his people and made sure they were happy and safe. However, he would never let anyone sail beyond the coral reef. "There is nothing beyond that reef but storm and rough sea," he would tell Moana.

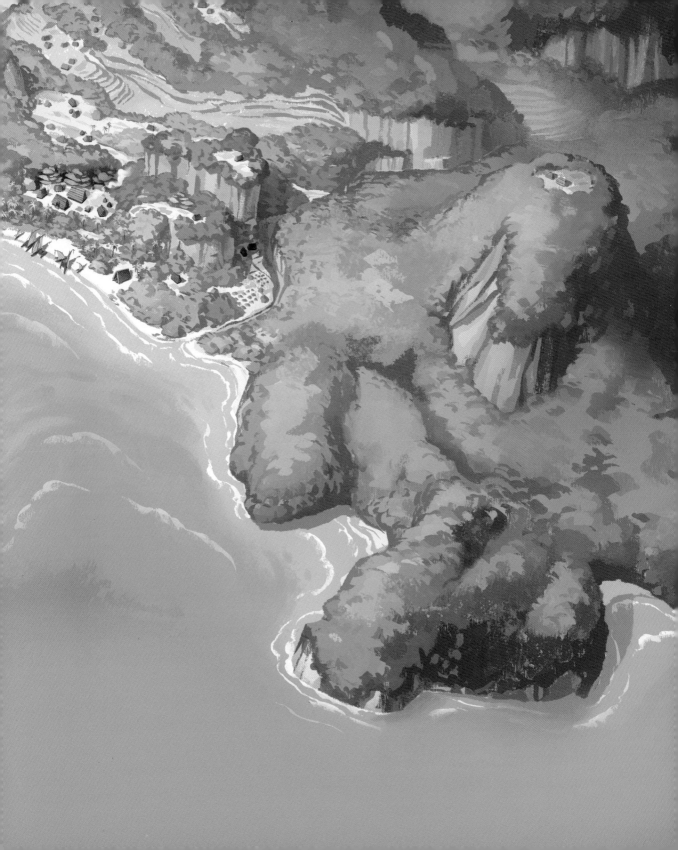

Gramma Tala used to tell Moana and her friends tales about their gods.
One story she'd always tell was about how Maui, a demigod with a
magical fish hook, stole the heart from the mother island, Te Fiti,
giving birth to a terrible darkness.

As Maui hurried from the island, he was attacked by a demon called
Te Kā. Te Fiti's heart and Maui's hook were lost in the ocean. "But one
day," added Gramma Tala, "the heart will be found by someone who
would find Maui, deliver him across the ocean to restore Te Fiti's heart
and save us all."

One day, Moana was playing on the beach and collecting shells. As she stepped into the water, it suddenly parted and rose up around her, creating a path further out to sea.

The little girl toddled along the path until she spotted a small, spiral stone. She grasped it in her hand and looked at it curiously. Just then, Chief Tui appeared. The sea quickly placed Moana safely back on the beach before her father arrived. "There you are," said Chief Tui. As he led Moana away, the toddler dropped the stone and forgot all about it.

As the years passed, Moana dreamed of a life on the waves, and would have spent every day by the sea if she could, but her parents taught her that she belonged in the village. "You must find happiness right where you are," said Chief Tui.

Moana enjoyed her life on Motunui. She helped the other islanders in any way she could, in the same way she would have to when she eventually followed in her father's footsteps and became chief.

When Moana was 16-years-old, Chief Tui took her to the highest mountain on the island. At the top of this was a large pile of stones. "One day, you will add your stone to this mountain," he said, "and raise our whole island higher."

"I'll lead the way," said Moana. "I'll have my people to guide me. We'll build our future together."

However, despite telling her father this, she was still drawn to the sea and looked out to the horizon from the mountain, wondering what adventures lay beyond.

That night, knowing Moana longed to sail the ocean, Gramma Tala led her granddaughter to a secret cave. "What's in there?" asked Moana.

"The answer," replied Gramma Tala, "to the question you keep asking yourself. 'Who are you meant to be?'"

Full of curiosity, Moana lit a torch and began to explore the cave. As the torch's flame flickered amongst the darkness, she came across a fleet of hidden boats!

Moana climbed up on one of the boats and hit a big drum. Suddenly, the history of her people flooded through her mind like a waterfall.

"We were voyagers!" cried Moana happily, as she leapt from the cave. She turned to Gramma Tala. "Why'd we stop?"

Gramma Tala explained that after Maui took the heart of Te Fiti, the ocean became a dangerous place. "To protect our people, the ancient chiefs forbid voyaging," she added.

Gramma Tala went on to explain that an evil darkness was starting to infect Motunui. Their home was in danger unless someone found Maui and took him to restore the heart of Te Fiti. It was then Gramma Tala revealed a spiral stone. It was the same stone Moana dropped when she was little. It was the heart of Te Fiti! "The ocean chose you," Gramma Tala told Moana.

Determined to save the island, Moana rushed to her father. "We have to find Maui!" she cried. "We have to restore the heart."

Her father was furious and took Moana to one side. "There is no heart," he said, snatching the stone from his daughter. "This is just a rock," he added, before throwing it to the ground.

As Moana picked up the spiral stone, she saw Gramma Tala's walking stick. But where was her grandmother? Suddenly, a villager appeared. "Chief," they said, worriedly. "It's your mother!"

Moana and her father raced to Gramma Tala's home and found her laying in bed. She was very sick. Moana knelt down beside her. "Go," said Gramma Tala, weakly. "You must. The ocean chose you."

"I can't leave you," protested Moana.

"There is nowhere you could go that I won't be with you," replied her grandmother, who gave Moana a necklace to hold the heart of Te Fiti. Using the last of her strength, she whispered, "Go."

Moana quickly packed some supplies and took one of the smaller boats from the secret cave. Sailing from the island, she looked up to the clear night sky and saw stars in the shape of the fish hook that Maui carried. Believing this was a sign, she decided to head in that direction. Suddenly, a fierce storm quickly rose up. WHAM! A giant wave crashed into her boat and everything went black.

Moana slowly opened her eyes as the sea splashed against her face. She had been washed up on the beach of a strange island. Looking around, she spotted the image of Maui's giant fish hook carved into the rock. There were also huge footprints in the sand. Moana realised this must be Maui's island!

Just then, Maui himself appeared! Summoning up all her courage, Moana said, "I'm here because you stole the heart of Te Fiti and you will board my boat, sail across the sea and put it back."

Maui was annoyed that Moana wasn't being more grateful. After all, he had stolen the heart so that humans would be able to create life themselves. "So," said Maui, "what I believe you were trying to say is *thank you*."

"Thank you?" asked Moana, who couldn't understand why the demigod was being so arrogant.

"You're welcome," replied Maui.

Maui then boasted about all the amazing things he had achieved. As he talked, he trapped Moana in a cave!

Maui wasn't interested in returning the heart. He only wanted to get his magical fish hook back. Without it he had been unable to shape-shift into the different animals that helped him travel from island to island. Now, using Moana's boat, he finally had a way to leave. He quickly set sail, leaving the young girl behind.

Moana wouldn't be put off that easily and quickly found a way out of the cave and dived into the water after Maui. Incredibly, the sea pushed her through the water at such a speed that she soon caught up with the demigod. Maui was surprised to see the ocean lift Moana up onto her boat.

"You will put back the heart!" Moana told Maui in her bravest voice, as she held the spiral stone out in front of her. But the demigod still refused to help. He was only interested in his fish hook and was desperate to get it back.

As the pair argued, spears and poisoned darts suddenly flew at them. They were under attack by Kakamora, tiny bandits dressed in coconut armour. Only by working together, were Moana and Maui able to fight off their attackers and escape.

After that, Maui finally agreed to help Moana with her quest to return the heart to Te Fiti. However, he insisted on fetching his fish hook first and he knew just where to look. "We go east," said Maui, "to the lair of Tamatoa."

As Maui prepared to set sail, the sea flicked one of the Kakamora's poisoned darts into his bottom. "Ouch!" cried Maui, as he fell to the floor, helpless. He now had no choice but to teach Moana how to steer the boat.

As he lay on the ground,
unable to move, he taught
Moana about 'wayfinding'.
This was all about how a sailor
uses the sun, stars, moon, wind,
waves and the currents to help
you get where you want to go.
Moana slowly but surely
learnt how it worked,
and felt closer to
her ancestors than
ever before.

By the next morning, the pair had reached a rocky island that was the entrance to Lalotai, the realm of monsters. Inside Lalotai was where they would find Tamatoa and Maui's fish hook.

Moana and Maui climbed to the top
of the island and eventually reached
the entrance. The only way into Lalotai
was to jump down a deep, dark opening.
So, they each took a deep breath and
jumped into the pitch-black hole.

Maui landed without any trouble
and quickly went hunting for his fish hook.

Moana, however, was caught by the tongue of a
huge monster and was unable to move! Suddenly,
an even bigger monster appeared and attacked
the one that had caught Moana. While the two
creatures fought each other, Moana was able to
escape and finally fell to the floor, unharmed.

As Moana looked for Maui, she went inside a cave and spotted his fish hook amongst a pile of shiny, gold objects! Surely getting the fish hook wouldn't be this easy? Suddenly the ground rose up to reveal… Tamatoa – who was a giant crab!

Tamatoa picked up Moana with his huge claw. "What are you doing down here?" he asked. Before Moana could reply, Maui appeared and grabbed his fish hook. The demigod tried to shape-shift but his powers weren't working properly. Tamatoa quickly dropped Moana and began to attack Maui!

Maui was pinned to the ground so, thinking quickly, Moana showed what looked like the heart of Te Fiti to Tamatoa. The stone glistened in the light. Tamatoa, who couldn't resist anything shiny, chased after her. As Moana ran away, she tripped and dropped the stone. However, her plan had worked and Maui was free. "We gotta go!" she cried.

"But the heart!" called out Maui.

"He can have it," replied Moana. "I've got this one." She opened her hand to reveal the real heart of Te Fiti. She had used an ordinary stone to trick Tamatoa! Before the angry crab realised he'd been fooled, a geyser of water exploded underneath the pair and launched them safely back out of Lalotai.

Back on the boat,
Moana helped Maui
practise shape-shifting
until he could do it again
easily. Confident they could
complete their quest, the pair
headed towards Te Fiti to return the heart.

Soon after, they spotted Te Fiti on the horizon. As they sailed nearer, the
demon Te Kā appeared and attacked them. Maui turned himself into
a huge hawk and, with the heart in his claws, tried to fly past the
gigantic monster. But the demigod was no match for Te Kā,
who swotted him out of the sky like a bug. Moana
helped Maui back onboard the boat, but both of
them were shocked to see Te Kā bring a
fist of fire down towards them.

The fist was going to destroy the boat when, at the very last moment, Maui raised his fish hook and blocked the devastating blow.

BOOM! The shockwave created a huge tidal wave that lifted Moana and Maui's boat and swept them far away from the monster's grasp.

Though Maui had saved them from Te Kā, their boat was badly damaged and the demigod's hook had a large crack in it. Maui was devastated. "Without my hook I am nothing," he said, sadly.

Angry at Moana, Maui used what power was left in the hook to shape-shift into a hawk and fly away, leaving her in the middle of the ocean, all alone.

Moana was heartbroken. She looked out across
the ocean, tears streaming down her face, and spoke
to the sea. "You chose the wrong person," she said.
"You'll have to choose somebody else." With that,
she held the heart of Te Fiti out to the sea.

After a moment, the water rose up and took the heart back below the waves. Moana was left with nothing and simply sat down and closed her eyes.

Suddenly, a magnificent, glowing manta ray swam beneath Moana's boat and she heard Gramma Tala's voice. As Moana opened her eyes and raised her head, she saw her grandmother's spirit was sitting on the boat with her!

Tala told her granddaughter that she would stay by her side, whether she decided to go home or carry on. As they spoke, hundreds of ghostly canoes filled with Moana's ancestors appeared. "Do you know who you are?" asked Gramma Tala.

Moana then realised returning the heart to Te Fiti had always been her destiny, so she dived into the water and recovered the spiral stone.

Back on board, she quickly repaired her boat and set sail for Te Fiti once again. Even without Maui, Moana was determined she would not fail this time, not with the history of her ancestors behind her and her grandmother's spirit by her side.

As Moana approached the island, Te Kā
appeared once more and hurled huge balls of
molten lava at her. Undaunted, Moana kept on sailing.

Becoming more and more angry, Te Kā raised its fist, but just before it
struck Moana, Maui appeared from out of nowhere and took the blow!
He had returned to help Moana, even though his hook was damaged.

With Maui distracting Te Kā, Moana was able to reach Te Fiti. But, when she arrived, all that was there was an empty crater where the island should have been. There was nowhere to put back the heart. Yet Moana didn't panic.

Looking back at Te Kā, she noticed a glowing lava spiral on the monster's chest. Its pattern matched the spiral-stone heart exactly. Moana knew what she had to do!

She calmly stepped into the sea and the water parted, creating a huge pathway between Moana and Te Kā.

"Moana!" cried Maui.
"What are you doing?"

Te Kā came thundering towards Moana, but stopped just in front of her. Despite the flames and angry look, the monster no longer seemed frightening to Moana. In fact, there was a sadness behind its eyes.

Moana reached out and placed the heart into Te Kā's chest. The green glow from the heart slowly began to spread across the monster's body.

Moana watched in amazement as the face of the lava monster transformed. With Te Fiti's heart restored, the mother island was changing back to her true self. A crown of flowers blossomed around Te Fiti's head and she took her place in the water. The island exploded back to life. There were lush, green leaves and beautiful plants. The mother island was back to what she once was.

Maui was so proud of Moana and gave her a big hug. Te Fiti had
also forgiven Maui for taking her heart and even fixed his hook for
him. Back on their boat the pair said their goodbyes, before Maui
shape-shifted into a hawk and flew away. Moana wasn't sad, as she
knew she would see Maui again one day.

Moana soon returned to Motonui, where her parents were so relieved to see their daughter return safe and sound.

Later that day, with a shell in her hand, Moana headed up the steps to the tallest mountain and proudly added it to the top of the pile of rocks shown to her by her father.

Moana finally knew who she was and she couldn't wait to explore
the oceans and lead her people on amazing new adventures!

THE END

COLLECT THEM ALL!

With 7 more exciting titles to choose from, you'll want to complete your Storytime Collection!

How far will a father go for his son?

Will Rapunzel learn who she truly is?

Will Simba ever become king?

Can Anna and Elsa stop an eternal winter?

Will Mowgli defeat Shere Khan?

Will the Incredibles save the day?

Will Belle be able to break the curse?